Homage to Cosmo

First published 1993
by Walker Books Ltd, 87 Vauxhall Walk
London SE11 5HJ

This edition published 1996

2 4 6 8 10 9 7 5 3

© 1993 Camilla Ashforth

This book had been typeset in Garamond.

Printed in Hong Kong

British Library Cataloguing in Publication Data
A catalogue record for this title is available
from the British Library.

ISBN 0-7445-4393-2

CALAMITY

Camilla Ashforth

WALKER BOOKS
AND SUBSIDIARIES
LONDON • BOSTON • SYDNEY

James and Horatio were
building a tower.
"One, two, three," said James
as he balanced the blocks.
"Seven, four," added Horatio.

"HEE-HAW!"

BUMP!

Something crashed into the Useful
Box and sent everything flying.

"What was that?" asked Horatio.
"It's a calamity," said James,
looking at the mess.
"What were you doing, Calamity?"
asked Horatio.
"Racing," Calamity said. "And I won."

"Can I race?" asked Horatio.

"Find yourself a jockey," Calamity said.

"Here's mine." She turned round.

But that's a bobbin, thought James.

He started to tidy up.

Horatio looked for a jockey.
I like this one, he thought.
It was James's clock.
"Are you ready?" asked Calamity.
They waited a moment.

"One, two, three, go!" Calamity
called. She hurtled round the
Useful Box. Twice.

Horatio tried to move his jockey.

He pushed it

and pulled it.

Then he rolled
it over.

His jockey would not budge.

Calamity screeched to a halt.

"Hee-haw! I won!" she bellowed.

"Let's race again."

James turned round.

He picked up Horatio's jockey.

"That's my clock," said James and he put it in his Useful Box.

Horatio looked for another jockey.

"One, two, three, go!" Calamity called.
She galloped very fast.
Backwards and forwards.

Horatio looked around.
I'll go this way, he thought, and
he set off with his new jockey.

"Hee-haw! Won again!" cried
Calamity, stopping suddenly.
Horatio looked puzzled.
"One more race," Calamity said.
"I'm good at this."

"James," whispered Horatio, "can
you help me win this time?"

"What you need is a race track," said James. "I'll make you one."

"This block is the start," he said.

"And this string is the finishing line.
Ready, steady, go!"

Calamity thundered off.
She was going the wrong way.

Horatio headed for the finishing line
as fast as he could.

Calamity turned in a circle and
headed back towards James.

"Stop!" James cried.

As Horatio crossed the line, Calamity collided with the Useful Box. CRASH!

"That was a good race. Who won?" asked Calamity.

"I think you both did," James said, and squeezed Horatio tight.

MORE WALKER PAPERBACKS
For You to Enjoy

HORATIO'S BED
by Camilla Ashforth

Horatio, the rabbit, has a problem: he can't sleep.
So his friend James, the bear, decides to make him a bed.

"Camilla Ashforth's gentle, object-packed water-colours lovingly suggest
an intimate world of mischief and tenderness."
The Times Educational Supplement.

0-7445-3156-X   £4.99

MONKEY TRICKS
by Camilla Ashforth

Shortlisted for the Illustrated Children's Book of the Year Award

The peaceful world of James and Horatio gets a lively jolt,
when the naughty monkey Johnny Conqueror appears on the scene!

"Picture book publishing at its best."
The Economist

0-7445-3168-3   £4.99

TEN IN THE BED
by Penny Dale

"A subtle variation on the traditional nursery song, illustrated with
wonderfully warm pictures … crammed with amusing details."
Practical Parenting

0-7445-1340-5   £4.99

Walker Paperbacks are available from most booksellers, or by post from B.B.C.S., P.O. Box 941, Hull, North Humberside HU1 3YQ

24 hour telephone credit card line 01482 224626

To order, send: Title, author, ISBN number and price for each book ordered, your full name and address,
cheque or postal order payable to BBCS for the total amount and allow the following for postage and packing:
UK and BFPO: £1.00 for the first book, and 50p for each additional book to a maximum of £3.50.
Overseas and Eire: £2.00 for the first book, £1.00 for the second and 50p for each additional book.

Prices and availability are subject to change without notice.